Harp O' Gold

BY Teresa Bateman

ILLUSTRATED BY Jill Weber

Holiday House / New York

To Benjamin, Daniel, Kraig, Doug, Sheila, Mike, and Laurie,
who know the power of music and love to share it with others
T. B.

For F. M. W. & R. M. W.
J. W

Text copyright © 2001 by Teresa Bateman
Illustrations copyright © 2001 by Jill Weber
All Rights Reserved
Printed in the United States of America

The text typeface is Golden Cockerell.

The artwork was painted with acrylic paint
and acrylic-based watercolors.

www.holidayhouse.com

First Edition

Library of Congress Cataloging-in-Publication Data
Bateman, Teresa.
    Harp o' gold / by Teresa Bateman; illustrated by Jill Weber.—1st ed.
    p. cm.
    Summary: A poor musician who dreams of riches and fame trades
his beloved but worn harp for one made of gold, but when he becomes
famous he finds that something is missing.
    ISBN 0-8234-1523-6
    [1. Fairy tales.] I. Weber, Jill, ill. II. Title.
PZ8.B30 15Har 2001   99-18821
[E]—dc21
CIP

Tom leaned back against an oak tree and plucked a melancholy air.

"The life of a minstrel," Tom complained to the sky, "is not what I had hoped."

He pondered this a moment. He had thought, as a young boy, of making music his livelihood. He would fill the land with his tunes, playing for both rich and poor, but mostly for the rich. They would sit in awe at his music, then fill his cap with gold. This, at least, had been his dream.

Reality, however, had proved harsher than expected.

Tom was a skilled minstrel. He put his heart into the music. Still, he had yet to play for anyone who could pay him more than a sack of flour, a few apples, or a blanket by the hearth. He enjoyed watching the music sweep his listeners away from their work-a-day worlds. He knew the music mattered to them. Still, he dreamed of wearing expensive clothes, riding a fine horse, and making friends with the rich and noble.

"It must be your fault," he said, only half jesting, to the harp. "You're hardly the instrument of a rich and successful minstrel."

He had received the old harp from his music teacher. It had seen many years of service, and they showed. The wood curved gracefully, but there was a gouge from a horse's hoof here, a chip missing there. The strings held true, however, and the music that flowed from the old harp seemed as seasoned as the wood that made it. Still, it looked old and worn.

"How could I hope to win a place by a rich man's fire with a poor man's harp?" Tom wondered aloud.

"I wish all problems were as easily solved," came a voice from the other side of the oak tree.

Tom nearly dropped the only instrument he had. When he turned, he found a man of very short stature, who swept his hat from his head and bowed.

"Sean O'Dell at your service," he said.

Ever polite, although somewhat confused, Tom stumbled to his feet. "What do you mean about solving my problem being simple?" he asked.

"Just what I said," replied Sean. "It seems you want a harp that shows where you wish to be, rather than where you've been. As it happens, I may have just the harp for you."

With that, the little man reached behind the tree and pulled out a truly splendid harp. The frame was made entirely of gold, and the strings glowed yellow in the sunlight.

Tom's eyes widened. With such a harp he would be welcome in any rich man's hall. "How much are you asking for that instrument?"

Sean smiled. "Why little and nothing. You'd be doing me a favor if you took it. All I'd ask in return would be the trade of that harp you have in your hand."

Tom could scarcely believe his good fortune.

"Done!" he cried, and gave over the old harp without a second thought.

He rested his new treasure against a shoulder and ran a finger lightly over the strings. They gave off a rather tinny, metallic sound, but his eyes were so caught up in the harp's glory that his ears ignored the truth.

"Thank you," he said, turning back to the little man, but he was gone as quietly and quickly as he had come, and the old harp was gone with him.

For a moment Tom felt a ping, as if a heartstring had been broken, but it passed.

Tom hurried on his way to the next town, sure of his welcome. For didn't he carry the best harp that had ever been seen?

His expectations proved true. When he put the golden harp to his shoulder in the town square, people gathered from all four corners to hear him play. To Tom the music seemed shallow and rather brittle. Still, that didn't seem to bother the crowd.

Soon he found himself at the town's finest inn, his room and board assured for the playing of that harp. The golden strings were beginning to make his fingers sore, but he played on long into the night, and people filled the room and bellowed for more.

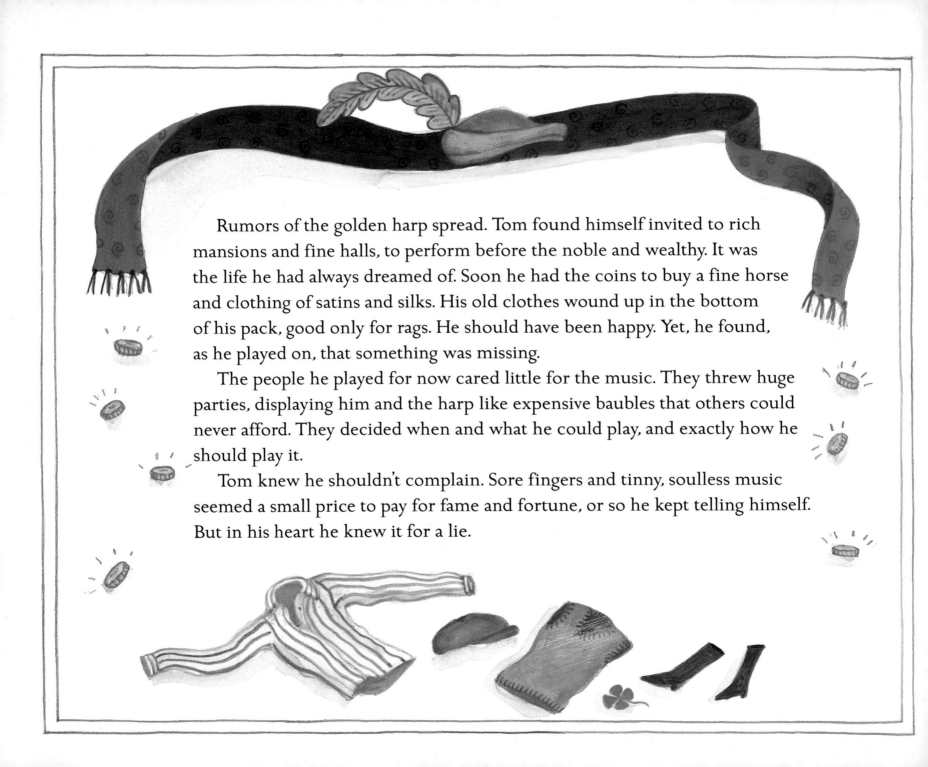

Rumors of the golden harp spread. Tom found himself invited to rich mansions and fine halls, to perform before the noble and wealthy. It was the life he had always dreamed of. Soon he had the coins to buy a fine horse and clothing of satins and silks. His old clothes wound up in the bottom of his pack, good only for rags. He should have been happy. Yet, he found, as he played on, that something was missing.

The people he played for now cared little for the music. They threw huge parties, displaying him and the harp like expensive baubles that others could never afford. They decided when and what he could play, and exactly how he should play it.

Tom knew he shouldn't complain. Sore fingers and tinny, soulless music seemed a small price to pay for fame and fortune, or so he kept telling himself. But in his heart he knew it for a lie.

Then the king himself commanded that Tom be brought to the palace.

Tom's spirits rose. Surely the king would appreciate the music for the music's sake. Tom practiced until his fingers ached and gave the king the best the harp o' gold had to offer.

The king smiled, hardly listening. So this was the minstrel and the harp o' gold that his nobles had been bragging about. Well, now that Tom was here at the palace, here he would stay. The harp o' gold would be the king's own treasure and none other would ever hear it again.

It took several days before Tom realized he was a prisoner at the palace. He was treated as an honored guest, yet when he tried to mount his horse and ride out the gate, he was quietly and politely turned back with one excuse or another.

Tom soon realized he would spend the rest of his life playing the harp o' gold before the king—playing what the king demanded, when he demanded it. He would have rich food and elegant clothes, but he wouldn't have freedom for himself, or for his music. His dream had turned into a nightmare.

Tom knew what he had to do. Late one night he dug deep into his pack and found the clothes he had been wearing when he had first received the harp o' gold. He shrugged into them, and they settled around him like old friends. He then tucked the harp o' gold into the worn pack.

Nobody recognized the thin, threadbare man as he walked past the guards at the kitchen gate and out into the night, leaving behind a fine steed and gold and silver coins.

It took Tom a fortnight to reach the forest again. At last he found the right tree and settled down with his back against it. Slowly he ran his fingers over the strings of the harp o' gold.

"I was wrong," he confessed humbly to the air. "I've learned my lesson. Please. What must I do to get my own harp back again?"

There was a long silence. For a moment Tom feared there would be no answer at all. Then he heard a whisper of music, and turned.

There, with Tom's old harp, stood Sean O'Dell. He ran his fingers lightly down the strings, then held it out, with a smile.

The harp o' gold fell to the ground, forgotten, as Tom reached for his old friend. His fingers curved to familiar strings. Lightly he played a gentle arpeggio. The sound resonated and filled an empty place in his heart.

Tom turned to thank Sean, but he and the harp o' gold were gone, as quickly and quietly as they had come.

Tom had no coins in his pockets and only the worn clothes on his back. If he were to eat tonight, he would have to find an inn or a farmhouse where he could trade his music for a meal. Yet never had he been happier.

Those who had known him before thought he had fallen on hard times. The rich and noble were no longer interested in this plain man with a plain harp, regardless of the wonderful music he could play. Tom didn't mind. There was more payment in the warm smiles and warmer hearts he found among those who loved the music for itself.

When he found someone who loved the music and the musician, he married and settled down to raise a family. His children often heard the tale of the strange instrument that had touched their father's life.

"Whatever happened to the harp o' gold?" they'd ask, and their father would smile and always reply the same.

"I sold it for a song, and I got the better bargain."